Surprise

A Message of Hope!

Robert James Karpie

Outskirts Press, Inc.
Denver, Colorado

Surprise
B4HEART
All Rights Reserved
Copyright © 2007 Robert James Karpie
V11.0

Cover Image © 2007 Robert James Karpie
All Rights Reserved. Used With Permission.

Cover Design © 2007 Robert James Karpie
All Rights Reserved. Used With Permission

Author Photo © 2007 Bob Mussell
All Rights Reserved. Used With Permission.

Outskirts Press
http://www.outskirtspress.com

ISBN-10: 1-59800-942-7
ISBN-13: 978-1-5800-942-2

Library of Congress Control Number: 2006938464

Outskirts Press and the "OP" logo are trademarks belonging to
Outskirts Press, Inc.

Printed in the United States of America

B4HEART

Humanity
Envisioned
And
Realized
Together

www.b4heart.com

Table of Contents

Synopsis

Two cousins, Chi and Jimmy, spend their summer vacation on their Grandpa's farm in Western New York and get the surprise of their life. It is a defining moment as they get enlightened, thanks to Oouey via B4HEART — Humanity Envisioned And Realized Together. For Oouey Gooey is a simple worm with a simple plan — Love!

He believes in miracles as he pursues his dream! He is but a blessing in a state of grace who, is opposed to drugs and devoted to peace. As an ambassador of hope and goodwill, he knows that 'Children', are out 'Future' and that 'Hardcore Rap Music' as well as aggressive video games and the glorification of acts of aggression portrayed via our main stream media; TV, movies, etc; have robbed us of a 'Generation of Progress', via violence, anger and hatred.

His mission is to start a revolution, a spiritual revolution to save mankind from greed, poverty, hunger, drugs, and corruption in the 'Name of

Humanity'. Intuitively, Oouey believes in a spiritual evolution — that someday mankind will in fact, be enlightened as we evolve to a higher state of 'Moral Consciousness'.

He is not a democrat or a republican but an Earthling with a wife named Olga and twenty-three offspring. They live in the 'Rose Garden' in Delaware Park in Buffalo, New York.

Oouey has a motto which he adopted from 'Peace Pilgrim'; "To Overcome evil with Good, falsehood with Truth and hatred with Love." He wants to spread these words-of-wisdom, world-wide; via dialog and interaction. But, Oouey needs your help? So, spread the word to all of your friends about his mission and his website!

Chi and Jimmy make a pact and take a vow with Oouey as they promise to B4HEART and Declare War on the 'Drug Epidemic', which is infecting our cities and schools and ruining Families. — **www.B4HEART.com**

This is the first in a series of Spiritual Enlightenment for the whole family, with work progressing quickly on the follow-up. It carries a 'Message of Hope' as it presents an opportunity with interactive substance, to make a difference; if you are willing to accept the challenge. It is both captivating and compelling as it demonstrates family and social values, little lessons in life.

'Surprise', will move and inspire both child and

parent as it entertains the simple joys of life --- Fun; Nature --- fishing, horsing around and worms; which leads to the ultimate surprise as Oouey prepares to make the world a better place for all to live in! Never underestimate the element of 'Surprise'.

About the Author

Robert James Karpie is a student of the human condition, wielding the written craft to enrapture the mind much like an artist wields a brush. The pages are a blank canvas on which to draw from a talent heralded by many and matched only by an imagination that rises to the task. 'Surprise', is but a fantastic journey from dream to inception, with persistence, faith and gosh darn guts!

Bob is a former U. S. Marine and has been married to his lovely wife Susan for over thirty-four years. They have two daughters and seven grand-children! Bob was born and raised in Buffalo, New York. He worked for the Buffalo Board of Education for twenty-three years as a computer operator at city hall.

At present, he owns B4HEART Publishing and www.B4HEARTplus.com. He is also the creator of www.B4HEART.com and he is a Preferred Author on www.writing.com/authors/b4heart. He is working on a novel entitled 'Social Security', which he intends on publishing shortly! He also has another short story for children ready to be published entitled: 'Mayan's Paradise'.

Preface

A little background: This book, *Surprise*, was inspired by the following story.

When I turned twenty-five, I had an epiphany, as I was sickened by what I was seeing in this world. It has been said that the world is a comedy to those who think and a tragedy to those that feel. Disgusted by inhumanity, I began expressing my thoughts on paper. I rattled on and on as if to clear my conscience, and I felt sorry for all mankind — humanity as a whole.

Unfortunately, nobody really cared, as most people are lost in their own little world with their own personal problems. In fact, some of my friends and family laughed at me like I was insane. Perhaps, I must admit, my writings were pretty bad, but with persistence, I managed to find my 'Muse.' I came to realize that mankind as a whole was a living bible, unfolding in time.

Ironically, I had to admit that we, all humans are little devils, as 'evil' is but 'Live', spelled backwards.

Everybody is guilty. 'Devil' is merely 'Lived', spelled backwards. It's a matter of wrong living. Ultimately, thanks to this epiphany, I view life as a matter of perspective and understanding, precisely --- 'Attitude', 'Attention' and 'Awareness'.

I concluded that we all hold destiny in our own hands via our actions as a whole; good actions verses evil actions. We could actually be little gods if we were willing to do angelic deeds. I was determined to make a difference, and share my insights but I didn't know where or how to start since nobody wanted to read the junk that I was writing. Thus, I would pray at night in bed for guidance; which led to 'The Dream'.

The Dream

One night, my thoughts were rambunctious as I fell into dreamland — lost, astray, deep in a dark, enchanting forest. Confounded by doubt and fear, I chose to flee from our world, since it was so cruel and corrupt. Drifting away, running scared, angry, confused, bewildered, and yet entranced by this mystical woodland, I shouted out loud — "Why, God? Why?"

Suddenly, I saw an incandescent light, particles of hope, dancing, peeking through the thick trees ahead of me. Curiously, I anxiously hurried toward that radiant area. The closer I came to this brilliant glow, the brighter it got.

Finally, I was out of the woods as I reached my focal point in a most beautiful Garden of Ether / Eden, which I could have never imagined. Astonished, as I assimilated my attitude, attention, and awareness, I knew that I was on Sacred Holy Ground, some harmonious realm — ineffable paradise.

Spellbound, I fell to my knees — mesmerized, amazed, overjoyed, and in a state of awe, beyond pure contemplation — exultation. Embraced by an exuberant feeling of Pure Perpetual LOVE —divine chemistry — I melted in rapture as I felt the presence of Sacred Holiness. My heart beat in tune with overwhelming yet soothing, soft music — bliss, which hailed from the Ultimate Divine.

Nonchalantly, I looked up into the sky, and there she was, totally refreshing and as clear as the full moon entertaining the darkest night; the Virgin Mary, Mother of Jesus, hovering amongst a cloud, floating closer and closer toward me. She was so beautiful, so immaculate — a bare testimonial of the absolute as a luminous white aura surrounded her completely. In fact, she looked as if she were made of light.

Ambushed by relentless peace, happy tears rolled down my face. Her elegance was so bright that I felt unworthy to look at her. I turned my head away. I wanted to stare, but I couldn't until she assured me; "Fear not, relax. Your heart is pure and you may look as your eyes won't hurt."

Ironically, she did not talk. Our minds — in fact, our thoughts — were engaged in communication as if by some visible sound waves, vibrating, emanating, and attracting and exchanging together as if magnetized. Mental telepathy!

She smiled and told me, "Your thoughts are true to your heart, and what you're thinking is right and just." Unfortunately, she warned, "time is running out, but the world isn't ready yet. Be patient. You will know when the time is right," she assured. Then she quoted Apostle Paul; "'Proclaim the Word; be persistent whether it is convenient or inconvenient...for the time will come when people will not tolerate sound doctrine.'"

She finished by encouraging me to do my 'Duty' in the Name of World Peace and Humanity. "Soon," she promised, "the World will be Ready, Willing, and Able as it is Desperate for Love; so Follow your Heart and Live your Dream!"

Overwhelmed and excited, in a state of ecstasy — an emotional overload of pure high — I awoke with water in my ears and salt in my mouth. I wiped the tears from my face and gently shook my wife to wake her up and tell her all about my Blessed Experience. Half asleep, she replied: "That's nice," and rolled over — back to sleep.

I was more determined than ever to make a difference. I realized that I couldn't run away from the troubles of the world any longer. Denial is evil. Denial is ignorant. I must rise to the occasion. I visualized Peace on Earth, in my mind's eye and vowed to do my best. It took a while but at last, I found my inner child — 'Oouey' —and I am determined to utilize him in the Name of Humanity to Spread the Word.

Shortly before that dream, my wife and I were with some friends at a flea market. I spotted an old painting; actually it was a beautiful lithograph of Baby Jesus and Mother Mary. It was lying on the floor in some corner. It was framed, but the glass was broken. I bought that old picture for $3.00. I hung it on my bedroom wall, as it inspired me. Twenty-five years have gone by, and it is still my inspiration.

Ye of Little Faith, thanks for the inspiration; for without your doubt, this book would never have happened.

This is the Painting that Inspired the Dream!

And the LORD God said, "Behold, the man is become as one of Us, to know good and evil; and now, lest he put forth his hand, and take also of the tree of life, and eat, and live for ever..."

(Genesis 3:22)

Acknowledgement

This book would not have been possible without the support of my family.

My seven grandchildren also inspire me daily by just being themselves.

Thanks Chi, Jimmy, Nickie, Nate, Mayan, Chey, and Timmy!

I Love All of You!

I would also like to thank my wife, Susan, and my two daughters, Brandie and Jamie, for all of their patience, love, understanding, and suggestions as this project has been an ongoing work in progress, which hopefully keeps on going and going and going! B4HEART

Humanity Envisioned And Realized Together

http://www.B4HEART.com

Believe & Pass It On!

Dedication

As life goes on, we live and learn how bittersweet it can be. Sometimes we get so lost in everyday living that we take it for granted? But we come to realize how much certain people mean to us as life is so precious. When we lose one of them, it is oh so painful. Therefore, I am dedicating this book to three such people who surely and clearly meant the world to me…

To my Father, James Karpie; who taught me the meaning of Love. To my son, William James Karpie, who died at the age of sixteen in 1990. And to my brother Dave, who was as close to me as two brothers can be; when we were growing up.

I Love and Miss All of You So Much!

Robert James Karpie

The Legend

It all started way, way back in the so-called 'Garden of Eden,' with Adam and Eve, who Oouey's Greatest Granddaddy, Ebenezer Worm (whose name implies Divine Help or Deliverance) tried but failed to warn and enlighten. For he attempted to prevent and later conquer evil as he stuck his neck out of 'The Apple' and shouted; "Excuse me, Madame," just before the 'Original Sin' or first bite.

But, Eve was so intoxicatingly engrossed, so enthused and relished in the process that she didn't notice or see him, and she almost bit Ebenezer's head off. In fact, Grampa Gooey was too slow, and he lost his tail in the inevitable act. Thus, 'Curiosity' is the 'Original Sin' that led to the 'Logical Fall of Mankind' per 'Choice' or 'Free Will'.

Some say it was a miracle that he didn't lose his life in this historic event. But, perhaps God did have mercy on poor ol' Gramps since he was on a sacred mission, actually trying to warn both Adam and Eve with a slice of advice. For he knew of God's little secret. He knew that if man indulged in the 'Apple of Good and Evil,' then man must also partake of the 'Tree of Eternal Life.'

Unfortunately, since he didn't succeed in averting the misdeed, evil manifested, and Grampa grew aghast. To make amends, he spent the rest of his life trying to get both Adam's and Eve's attention. But, they were too proud and salacious to listen as evil persisted and escalated.

Thus, on his deathbed, in front of his entire family, he made them all promise and take a solemn vow to erase evil and pass the word on to their offspring. Hence, Oouey believes that he was deemed by fate as a duty to fulfill his Greatest Grampa's death wish — to avenge the 'Logical Fall of Man.'

Chapter 1
Planting Seeds

Chi and Jimmy are inseparable cousins who fight like cats and dogs. "Typical!" That's what Pa always says. "Brotherly Love; God help anybody who messes with one when the other is around. They'll take on the world when they become teenagers as a force to be reckoned with."

Pa is proud of his two grandsons. They have been spending their summers with him since they were two and a half and three, five years now. The little "Tigers" are six months apart, and the older they get, the more independent they become. Sometimes they think they know everything about anything.

Sometimes Pa calls them "Smarty-pants." That is his way of getting their attention as he tries to get his point across; food for thought. Pa believes in teaching by example, but he also makes it fun and interesting as he inspires a positive attitude.

Sometimes Pa will instigate trouble just to get Chi and Jimmy mad at each other so they wrestle and toughen up. But, watch out if he just picks on one. It is a sight to see as they gang up and tackle him.

Pa just laughs it off as he teaches them the secret of push and pull, as well as pressure points. After all, Mr. Gravity is a major force to reckon with, when it comes to self-defense. From experience, Pa has the battle scars to prove it.

The boys love their Grandfather, and he adores them. It is a mutual respect. They all vowed to stick together as Pa taught them the values of loyalty, trust, honesty, and teamwork.

Pa always preached, "Count your 'Blessings' and be 'Thankful' as success is overrated. Your health, family, and friends are precious, and 'Love', is the essence of life. Love is Sacred. Love is Divine. God is Love!"

Chi and Jimmy agreed with Pa. They always agreed with him, even though half of the time they didn't know what he was talking about. Gramma would just shake her head in disbelief. "They're only kids!" she would remind him.

But, Pa knew what he was doing. He was just investing in the future via his procreations. Pa was making a difference in his own way. He knows that children are our greatest natural resource, the key to humanity.

"Eventually, it will all sink in," he would snap back at Gram, his wife. For Pa knows that they are little sponges that absorbed without thinking. He was just planting seeds.

After all, he was a farmer. It is a right-brain thing as children are in tune with the infinite. Their innocence is not yet corrupted by logic. He was merely laying a foundation as he set the standards. Intuitively, Pa has a dream; and his offspring are extensions of that dream en route to destiny.

"Someday," Pa predicted, "mankind will believe in God, himself, and each other! But until then, we will never have 'World Peace'. Trust and cooperation are both vital to the cause."

He only hopes that he lives long enough to see his dream come true. He is determined to give guidance, direction and moral support for his cause, a solid foundation. Together, Pa knows that he and his two grandsons can make a difference as every little good deed helps.

Thus, Pa taught the boys his Marine Corps motto --- Semper Fi (Simper Fidelis or Always Faithful). He assured them that if they were faithful to God, themselves and the rights of others; then they would be doing their part to make the world a better place for all to live in.

"Far too many worry about their own rights and forget their responsibilities to others? We have moral obligations!" Pa was adamant.

Both Chi and Jimmy wanted Pa's dream fulfilled, so they vowed to do their best. Pa encouraged the boys to follow their dreams. "If you believe," he assured them, "you'll achieve! Never underestimate the Power of your 'Dreams'! Focus and set your goal; desire and intent are the keys to turning them into reality!"

"Faith is your 'Inner Strength'. It's better to live your dream than dream it!" Pa explained that all of us have a purpose in life. "Find a need and fill it! Define your purpose, and proceed with passion!"

"I want to be an astronaut!" Chi exclaimed.

"And I want to be a superhero!" Jimmy interrupted.

"Go for it!" Pa inspired their confidence. "Never give up. 'No' and 'Rejection', are but facts of life; small obstacles that you can overcome. Sometimes, you gotta try a little bit harder! Adversity; makes you stronger. Be prepared! Always do your homework. Keep your ears and eyes open as well as your mind and heart. Everybody is born with potential!"

"Pa...pa...patential?" Jimmy stuttered, all confused with a puzzled look on his face.

"Potential, Jimmy." Pa and Chi laughed as he corrected him. "It means possibilities. We all have talent, but everyone must find his own passion, his burning desire, his very reason for being.

"Unfortunately, far too many go through life bewildered, lost in hurry and worry, all confused as life can be so overwhelming. Sometimes they get sidetracked by jealousy, envy, or regret as they feel sorry for themselves."

"Me and Jimmy thought we were lost in the woods once," Chi interrupted, "but you fooled us, as you were watching all the time."

"Yeah, it was scaarry," Jimmy agreed. "I thought I saw lions, tigers, and bears."

"Yeah," Chi agreed. "Spooky, we felt sorry for ourselves!"

"That's my job, to keep an eye on you two boys, but you better be careful, as I can't be there all of the time," Pa warned. "Sometimes life can seem scary, but you must learn to overcome your fears. Sometimes your imagination will play tricks on you!"

Both Chi and Jimmy shook their heads in agreement with Pa as they felt brave at that moment.

"Sometimes," Pa continued, "life will sneak up on you and bite you on your behind. Sometimes it will knock you on your behind! Unfortunately, shit happens."

The boys giggled since Pa swore but, he continued anyway; "When shit happens, just deal with it. When 'Grace', happens, enjoy it! If and when you get knocked on your ass, just get back up and try, try, try again. A 'Little Humbling', is 'good for the soul; apply yourself, 'Perseverance'!"

"Persir, what?" Chi was lost.

"Learn from your mistakes." Pa enlightened. "Life is full of disappointments but, don't you become a disappointment. Don't take life for granted. Life is full of surprises. You never know what you can accomplish, discover or learn until you try."

"You must remember that there is always 'HOPE'. Nobody knows what tomorrow will bring. Have 'Faith', be 'Patient', be 'Ready' and never underestimate or doubt your 'Ability'! Be true to yourself. If you give up, your dream dies." Doubt is a curse; it kills dreams."

Chi and Jimmy promised to try to remember what Pa had told them as he tucked them in bed and kissed them both good night. Then Pa reminded them of what Jesus professed: "Seek and you will find, ask and you will receive, knock and the door will open."

Pa got up --- off the bed to turn the light off. They exchanged good-nights, again. He smiled as the boys giggled and goofed around as he was about to leave the room and encouraged: "Pleasant Dreams!"

Suddenly, Jimmy sat up straight and asked; "Pa, is dre...dre...dreamland re...re...real?"

Pa laughed as he sat back down on the edge of their bed. Then he replied, "Dreamland is as real as life it self, but it is a 'Magical Place'. It is more important than we can ever imagine as it deals with our inner nature. In fact, 'Dreams' have fascinated artists, puzzled scientists and laymen since the beginning of time.

'Why do people dream", Chi asked curiously.

"We all have 'Dreams' and we all dream", Pa answered. "It is definitely a natural phenomenon but nobody knows why for sure. It has something to do with our subconscious awareness and memories. Dreams are a source of 'Secret Knowledge'. They hold lessons, provide insight and have produced source material for some of Humanity's most magnificent creations."

"Your Gram's sewing machine is the result of a dream and Shakespeare wrote about his dreams. Thomas Edison used his dreams to work out details of his inventions and, at least one dream was responsible for a Nobel Prize. All dreams carry a message, even a nightmare. Frankenstein was inspired by a dream as the author Mary Shelley, dreamt about 'It' --- 'Frankenstein'."

"Wow!" The boys were amazed.

"In dreamland, you are in charge of your dreams and you can dream about anything you want to. You can be anybody or anything that you want to be. In dreamland you dream your dreams. But in life, if you 'BELIEVE' and work hard at it; you will 'Live' your 'DREAM!" Pa was adamant and then, he told the boys about his 'Blessed Dream'.

They were surprised! They knew that he had 'A Dream', but they never heard about 'The Dream'! When Pa finished, Chi and Jimmy were both amazed as they pondered and drifted off into 'Dreamland'.

Chapter 2
Family Tradition

Gram knows how to get Pa's goat, really make him sort of mad. She has a bad habit, like most Grams do, as she will always rescue the boys when they get in trouble. Pa just shakes his head and walks away when that happens.

"Accountability, accountability, accountability," he would shout back. Pa knows how to influence and he knows that discipline starts at home. But, so does Love, understanding, care, concern, respect and trust. Thus, he believes in both discipline and self-discipline. He practices what he preaches. "You guys are responsible for your actions. You must pay the consequences!"

Gram would smile, and the boys would giggle in an effort to butter him up. But, if Pa was real mad, he'd call them a couple of 'sissies,' and they knew to shut right up. Even Gram knew that that was when he meant business. For when Pa was serious, it was best to let him cool off by himself.

As usual, he'd head for the old barn and indulge in his cider barrel. He was proud of his orchard, and he usually won the cider competition at the State Fair. Cider making was his hobby, and he savored every drop. In the winter, Pa and Gram would drink hot cider laced with cinnamon, together with cookies laced with 'Love', by the fireplace.

The boys couldn't stand it when Pa was upset, so they always gave him about fifteen minutes to unwind. Then they would creep into the big ol' barn and hide. They knew that Pa would forgive them. He always did.

Pa would pretend not to see them. Usually, by then he would just be finishing his mug of cider and then go to the spiracle to get some more. For some odd reason, that barrel never went empty, but Pa would always complain.

"Who was drinking my cider?" He'd scratch his head and bend down on his knees to watch it pour out. "Somebody has been drinking my cider. Just look how slow it is pouring out!"

The boys couldn't help but laugh out loud, as they couldn't wait to play their little game. They would stumble out like two drunken sailors, and Pa would charge at them, and they would whip him.

Gram was always in the doorway of the barn, shaking her head in disgust as she didn't like the idea of them imitating alcohol. "Relax!" Pa would always try to calm her down as he went to his cabinet to get three more mugs — one for Gram, one for Chi, and one for Jimmy.

Pa would then pour the drinks as everybody giggled in anticipation as he passed them out, one at a time, and asked, "What shall we toast to?" The boys couldn't wait to shout "Gramma!"

Poor Gramma is famous for her Toot-Toot, and the boys never let her forget it. Neither did Pa as they all cheered, "Tooty-Tooty Gramma!" It is a 'Family Tradition'.

Gram would graciously laugh and smile. She has a 'Great Sense of Humor'. After all, she always insists that laughter is a beautiful thing; especially, if and when you can laugh at yourself honestly.

Pa and the boys Love their Gram. She is a good sport and besides, she is an expert when it comes to picnics, mud-pies, butterflies and kite-flying. She knows all about the birds and the bees, honey and flowers. She is the best nurse who always kisses, cleans, and bandages your boo-boos. And she surely knows how to cook and clean, sew and bake brownies.

She even likes to fish and Gram is the 'Champ', when it comes to skipping stones. When they go camping at Allegany State Park, she tells spooky stories by the camp-fire. And, somehow, Gram always knows what you are thinking, before you ask? But, she always seems to worry about them. They just laugh it off when she reminds them to "'Be Careful', 'Enjoy Your Day' and 'Wake Up and Smell the Roses'?"

Chapter 3
Quality Time

Cats and dogs littered the barnyard. Pa didn't want any 'undesirables' as he would call them — rats. "One or two is okay," he'd say, "perhaps a family, but no more! Varmints are varmints."

Pa isn't prejudiced. He taught the boys to respect all of God's creatures. But sometimes, enough is enough. "Beware of the human rats," he warned with a smile as the boys laughed.

"Beware of people who pretend to be your friends. They have ulterior motives. Ironically", Pa continued, "the 'Human-Race', has turned 'Life' into a 'System', which evolved into a 'Rat-Race'. Far too many people are so self-centered, so engrossed in me – me - - me and my --- family? Unfortunately, they have a blatant disregard for 'Humanity', wanton arrogance; selfish priorities?"

"To add insult to injury, 'Humanity' suffers because the 'System', is so corrupted. The deck is stacked against most people in this world. Sometimes, humans have to cheat in order to survive? Earth has become a vicious circle of a dog eat dog world. Therefore, it is our duty to change the 'Wicked System'. Mankind must reach out via 'Love' and help, share and care about each other!"

The boys respected Pa's opinions; 'Little Facts of Life' as he called them. Pa had a way of pointing out both the good, and the bad in people. Chi and Jimmy absorbed what they could. They liked hanging out with him, as he always has something to say or teach them about. Sometimes he is funny, but they learned that there is a time for work and a time for play.

Somehow, Pa always manages to make work fun. He encourages the boys to enjoy life and make the best out of each task. "Take pride in your work," he always reminds them, "for somebody has to do it!"

"Life is an adventure", he assured; "everyday is a "Blessing". Jump in and get involved. Take an interest and commit yourself. There are 'Heroes', all around us --- 'Teachers', 'Nurses', Policemen' and 'Firemen', just to name a few. They serve Humanity, via Love; their Love to 'Make a Difference'! They take 'Pride', in their work! They know that 'Society' depends on them. They inspire 'Hope', by doing their job and that 'Hope', keeps 'Dreams', alive, by helping, sharing, teaching and or by saving lives!"

By the way, Pa, Chi, and Jimmy have a special task

that they Love to do. It is called 'Worm Patrol'. It is a search and rescue mission and the boys are always ready, willing, and able to participate. Thus, they can't wait for an early summer morning downpour and hope that it will clear up soon, as that is when the fun begins. For that's when the worms like to come out and play. "Naturally", Pa always told them that; "worms liked to dance in the rain." Don't you?

Unfortunately, some of them got so engrossed and intoxicated in the pleasure of splashing in puddles as they wandered, from puddle to puddle, that they actually got lost and confused when the sun came out and dried out all the rain, baking them alive as they were stranded on a long, hot sidewalk or driveway.

That's when Pa and his partners would come to the rescue of the poor unfortunate creatures that were helplessly waiting, anticipating death. Both Chi and Jimmy would get the biggest kick out of picking one up gently and rubbing his tiny belly as they made eye contact. If a worm looked all dried up, then they would spray that worm with some H2O. They would always tell each worm: "Don't worry fellow, we're just trying to help you!" But sometimes the little worms would get so scared that they would poop in their hands.

The boys and Pa giggled and laughed as they chased each other with yucky hands, trying to wipe the worm poop on each other's clothes. Goofing off made their angelic adventure even more fun as they suspended disbelief and Pa excited their imagination by sparking an interest, a little human intervention.

For he influenced their 'Sense of Wonder'; the 'Awe and Wonder of Being'; the 'Gracious Mysteries of Life'!

Gram would just shake her head and laugh when they came home all gooey and muddy. She was proud of Pa for letting the boys enjoy some simple joys of life. After all, Nature is the perfect opportunity for bonding. Nature is the ultimate mentor. Laughter and Nature go hand in hand --- Free Fun!

Sometimes, Pa would tell the boys that the worm actually winked at them as a way of saying "Thank you!" Unfortunately, neither Jimmy nor Chi ever saw it. But Pa insisted and teased them that they weren't paying attention. Perhaps, he suggested, it was because they were afraid to kiss the little fellow good-bye.

Habitually, Pa always preached that man is blinded by fear and doubt. But the boys had no doubt as to how appreciative the little worms were. For it was a sight to be seen; as they literally dove in the ground, as soon as they were released in some soft mud or grass. It was like a game of 'hide n seek'; catch me if you can, again --- next time!

Incidentally, it was Jimmy who made Pa laugh. He got brave one day and insisted that a worm winked at him. Chi had no choice as he also kissed one of the worms; good-bye and swore that that worm winked at him too. Perhaps he was curious as he believed Pa and Jimmy, or perhaps he didn't want to be called chicken; peer-pressure.

So he gave the worm a little 'Lovin'. After all, Pa always said, "Never underestimate the 'Power of Love'! Never underestimate the 'Power of Suggestion'."

Pa laughed again, as he cherished their precious moments together. He remembered the first time he saved a worm. He was pleased that his grandsons enjoyed their little mission of mercy as he passed the tradition on to the next generation.

Together, they got involved, connected with Nature and made a difference by saving a few lives. Actually, they were doing God's work, as God does work in mysterious ways. "Man is but an instrument of God!" Pa exclaimed.

"Sometimes," he assured, "all creatures, big or small, need a helping hand. Most of the time many humans need a helping hand. All you have to do is take a look around. There are a lot of homeless people, all over this world."

"Far too many are down and out, tired, weak and weary." Pa tried to get his point across. "They have nobody to turn to for help? So they just give up in spite of the fact that everybody wants to be 'Loved'? Nobody wants to be forgotten or left alone. Sometimes, people just need a shoulder to cry on or somebody to lean on."

"Unfortunately," Pa continued, "many humans don't seem to care or take or make the time for 'Love'. Ironically, lots of people are afraid to ask for help. Sometimes they are too proud, sometimes they feel ashamed, but regardless, 'A friend in need is a friend indeed,' as a sense of accomplishment — the deed or act itself that may make you feel alive and realize the value of living."

The boys listened to Pa when he talked because he always made them think. Sometimes he talked in riddles, and other times he made no sense at all; at least not at that moment. But they came to realize that he knew what he was talking about, at least when it came to fishing, fighting, worms, dreams, dreamland and yellow snow. After all, Pa graduated from the School of 'Hard Knocks'!

One time when they were on 'Worm Patrol,' Pa told the boys that an infamous man named Charles Darwin proclaimed that "there is no animal which has played a more important part in the history of the world than the earthworm." (Charles Darwin's *The Formations of Vegetable Mold Through the Action of Worms*.)

Pa explained that "Darwin recognized the value of the earthworms and their tilling as well as their divine poo-poo, better known as topsoil." The boys giggled and were glad that they weren't wiping real poop on each other. They were proud that they were playing an important part in the history of the 'World' as they helped the worms; so they could still do their job.

To them, it is 'Cool' to get involved. Pa is 'Cool', as are the worms. But Pa shared an insight as he enlightened them with a little advice. He proclaimed that: "'Truth' is akin to 'Cool' as both are repulsive to the 'Un'."

They were perplexed? They didn't quite understand until Pa explained that 'Cool', is being real; true to yourself as well as to others. "Unfortunately," Pa continued, "People that are not 'Cool', will often be jealous or laugh at you as they are either ignorant or afraid of 'Truth'."

"Sometimes," he elaborated, "the 'Truth' hurts! You must face your self. You got to know who you are and what you stand for. If you don't respect your self, you cheat your self, and then, why should others respect you? It ain't 'Cool' to lie to or fool your self!"

"Never," he warned, "Never use or abuse anybody. Don't talk about people, behind their backs. Don't hate and don't poke fun at or put anyone down, because they are different than you are or because they are 'Un – Cool'."

The boys promised to be 'Cool' and, Pa believed them! But he warned them that, "'Cool People', don't hang out with fools and 'Cool People' don't need drugs! Fools do drugs?"

Chapter 4
The Surprise

Chi and Jimmy were doing their early morning chores, as life on a farm entails responsibility. First they would attend to the chickens so Gram could get breakfast started. Next, the cows, which they liked milking. Sometimes they'd have a milk war as they actually squirted each other. It was fun! Especially if it was a cold morning, as the warm milk felt --- warm.

One time, Pa caught them in the act. He seemed mad; however, he couldn't help but snicker. He told them to quit goofing off, or else! They always wondered, *Or else what?*

Neither of them ever worried, as they had their ace in the hole. Gramma would surely save them from 'or else'. They just laughed it off. But deep down, they knew what consequences were as they had both paid the price more than once. Sometimes you learn right from wrong the hard way.

Both Chi and Jimmy were afraid of milking the nanny goat. She was very moody. Sometimes she liked to kick, and it hurt. Sometimes Billy, the male goat, would get jealous, sneak up, and bite you on the behind. He didn't like anybody messing with his spouse except Pa.

After breakfast, the boys went fishing at the big watering hole. Gram packed them a lunch and told them to be careful. They promised, but reminded her that they both could swim like little fish. After all, Pa threw them in when they were three and a half and four and wouldn't let them out until they mastered the art of water survival. He taught them not to fear water but respect it.

Chi and Jimmy were always proud when they brought the fresh fish home for dinner. Pa taught them to respect the fish and life. "Keep those that you want to eat and let the others go free." He set the Law of Nature in their minds. Pa proclaimed that "greed was evil, and waste was just as bad."

He warned them not to be overcome by greed. "Don't," he'd always preach, "don't let greed become you!" He explained that, "there is a lot of evil in this world, which evolved into corruption. Unfortunately, there are a lot of people in this world who ignore or fell prey as they cooperate with evil. Therefore, there are a lot of people that are starving because of denial."

"Far too many are poor!" Pa would cry with a tear or two in his eyes. For it made him mad, as poverty is so sad — a harsh reality, as life is not fair. Thus, both

Chi and Jim learned the value of sharing and caring as Pa told them that, "life is but a matter of survival and that all people just want to be 'Happy'".

He declared that; "everybody has a 'Right to Life', 'Liberty' and the 'Pursuit of Happiness'. But", he continued; "how can you be happy with no food in your belly or when you don't know where you are going to sleep tonight? True happiness", Pa insisted, "is an 'Inner Peace'; a feeling you get by helping others!"

"Be grateful, thankful, for all that you are blessed, with. Be aware of the less fortunate, of what they don't have or need. Don't be afraid to share. Mother Nature will provide but, we must learn to cooperate with 'Her' and each other. Together, humans can conquer evil poverty!"

They cleaned the fish on the old table by the dock. Then they horsed around respectfully in the water before they headed back. Gram was pleased with the catch and suggested the boys go raid Pa's cider barrel and take a nap in the barn before dinner.

The boys obliged, sort of, but had no intentions of taking a nap. They went there to chill out. They fought over who was going to pour first. They got so tired from wrestling, that they just fell fast asleep. Perhaps Gram knew best after all.

Jimmy woke up first. He was thirsty as thirsty can be. He poured his drink from the cider barrel. But something wasn't quite right as he heard a slight plop. Startled, he couldn't believe what he was seeing.

He put his mug on the floor and double-fisted his eyeballs, grinding the sleep-bugs away. He took another peek, a triple-take as he looked away several times. But it was still there. He stared with disbelief.

Jimmy got down on his knees to investigate. It was a big ol' worm, floating on his back. He was amazed as they made eye contact.

The worm stared right back at him with huge, red bloodshot eyeballs that pierced his soul. Ironically, he wasn't just floating anymore. He was splashing away, doing the backstroke!

Elated, it popped up his head, burped, winked at Jimmy, and said in a pleasant voice: "Hey, hey, hey, salutations; it's your lucky day! Have no fear, Oouey is here; Oouey Gooey at your service!"

Jimmy was so astonished, he jumped to his feet. He didn't know what to do, so without hesitation, he woke up his cousin. Chi couldn't believe his eyes or his ears, as he was awed with open-mouthed observation — surrealism.

Oouey said, "Hello." It was both breathtaking and mind- boggling.

He was not very dashing or elegant-looking — quite contrary to it, as he was pure ugly. But who were they to judge? After all, isn't beauty 'skin-deep' or, as they say, 'in the eye of the beholder,' as God works in strange ways. The boys heard stories about miracles but, a talking worm? Was this a divine spontaneous appearance, or perhaps a blessing in disguise?

He spoke with authority, which commanded their reluctant attention. His influence was a matter of utmost concern, precisely the difference between life and death — his. Both Chi and Jimmy had grasped this profound truth without any doubt, but were they dreaming?

It was a most unusual confrontation, an absolute impossibility. They were about to converse with a worm. Suddenly, Oouey shouted, "Get me out of here, please, if you will."

Chi picked up the big mug and poured the cider on the wooden floor. Oouey bounced and rolled and coughed and screamed and gagged and gasped — "Good grief!", after he caught his breath. Then he thanked them sincerely from the bottom of his HEARTs.

"You're welcome!" they echoed as they laughed in delight.

"How'd you get in there?" Jimmy asked curiously.

"I fell in," he admitted stupidly. "I wanted some of your Pa's cider."

"Awesome, you know Pa!" Chi was surprised. "You got a mustache just like him."

"We're old Pals!" Oouey left it at that as he did not elaborate. "Your Pa has a mustache like me! He likes my style!"

"Where are you from?" Jimmy was nosey.

"I live in The Rose Garden in Delaware Park next to the Lincoln Memorial in Buffalo, New York," replied Oouey as the boys were anxious. "It's a beautiful place, our little paradise."

"That's pretty far away from here!" Chi was sharp.

"Yeah, at least a thousand miles," Jimmy put his two cents in as he had no concept of distance.

Oouey laughed repeatedly. "Not quite that far, Jimmy. Maybe sixty-five miles, give or take a few." Oouey corrected his innocent ignorance.

"You know my name!" exclaimed Jimmy with excitement.

"Yepper. I know of your whole family."

"Cool!" The boys responded simultaneously as they were all 'Ears'.

"How did you get here?" asked Chi "You got a Worm-Mobile or something?"

Oouey Gooey chuckled. "Jeepers, oh gosh no!" he replied. "It's really quite simple but somewhat complicated for a logical mind to understand."

The boys were confused as they weren't ready for a

sophisticated lecture, but Oouey gave them the heads-up anyway. He knew that they weren't brainwashed yet.

"Worm-Holes," he continued; "Quantum-leap, astral-projection, a virtual reality on Earth as well as in the entire universe. It is when you make a hyperspace connection, a divine alignment, as the brain is both a transmitter and a receiver. Actually, it's a perfect example of Psycho-kinesis — mind over matter."

"I'm proud to be a master of it, as reality is mind-boggling. Consciousness is limited only by fear and doubt as the past is but a prelude to now. For life is but a vast array, a continuous electromagnetic spectrum of vibrating energy — heat, light, and sound."

"Cool!" they echoed again mesmerized, as they scratched their heads with fascination.

"Can you teach us?" asked Chi

"Maybe," Oouey wasn't so sure; as time and space are beyond the conception of humans. "You are limited only by your own imagination? It's up to you. You control your own destiny."

"De…de…dessstiny?" Jimmy stuttered.

"Fate, divine decree," Oouey tried to explain. "Life is full of 'Surprises', you choose your own path. It is a challenge, full or risks and rewards. Everyday is a gift! You must learn to enjoy the ride. You got to wake up and smell the roses. 'Seek and you will find, ask and you will receive, knock and the door will open.'"

"That's what Gram and Pa always tell us!" Jimmy was proud.

"How'd you get so smart?" Chi asked.

"I'm a bookworm who loves to hang out at www.writing.com. Reading makes you smart. It makes you think. It is food for your brain. I utilize my cosmic sense, my intuition. Humans are lost in common sense, or shall I clarify — logic."

"Did you come from Mars in some kinda spaceship?" Jimmy couldn't comprehend.

"Actually, I'm an 'Earthworm'. That makes me an 'Earthling'. I Love 'NASCAR', 'Football', 'Bull Riding', 'Rock n Roll', 'Country Music' and 'Hockey'! I Love the Buffalo Sabres! But," he continued, "I'm also a celestial being with clairvoyance as an exalted state of consciousness."

"I see auras, spirits, and deities. Love is my passion. Humanity is my dream, my destiny. My mission is to save the world from poverty, greed, and drugs and wipe out hunger once and for all."

"Can we help you?" Chi asked sincerely.

Oouey clapped his little hands and jumped with

joy, as he was so pleased! "But of course. But we need a plan."

"We can go fishing!" Jimmy got so excited with his idea.

"Uh?" Oouey gave him the 'Evil-Eye' as he almost had a HEARTs attack. "Fish food?" He thought out loud. "I haven't any desire to sacrifice myself in suicide. No thank you!"

Jimmy was disappointed until Oouey assured him that they could become 'Fishers of Men'.

"We'll start a grass-roots effort," he suggested. "Pro-action! It'll be a revolution, a spiritual revolution. We'll recruit the young and old, anybody and everybody that cares."

"The more the merrier," Oouey was adamant; "but we need real people, people who believe in B4HEART! Effort is the key. United, we shall conquer evil poverty!"

"B4HEART?" The boys mumbled in confusion.

"People who are willing to be for — Humanity Envisioned And Realized Together. We need action, not promises. Promises don't feed the hungry. People starve waiting for promises to be fulfilled."

"Action speaks louder than words. Talk is Cheap. Broken promises are costly, as time and space are but conditions and environment, an awareness as you are a witness to and participant of organic being. All life revolves around 'Choices' --- 'Cause and Effect', as every action has a reaction!"

"Anybody," he continued, "who ignores poverty and hunger is a fool. I despise their excuses. I pity fools. They are starving spiritually and are a disgrace to the 'Human Race'. They are but lost souls. Inhumanity is nonsense, pure foolishness?"

"Love is the 'Answer'", Oouey assured! "Love is the 'Way'! God is Love! When you engage in 'Love Mode', you become one with God! Love is the literal origin of virtual energy. Hence, LOVE is the acronym for --- Literal Original Virtual Energy.

"Wow!" The boys were amazed but, Pa enlightened them all about Love and God. Thus, they could relate to 'Virtual Energy' or 'LOVE'.

"Do all worms want to help mankind?" Chi asked.

"In many ways," Oouey assured, "but I have a special mission! It all started way, way back in the Garden of Eden, with Adam and Eve, — whom my Greatest Granddaddy, Ebenezer Worm (whose name implies 'Divine Help' or 'Deliverance') tried but failed to warn and enlighten. For he attempted to prevent and later conquer evil as he stuck his neck out of 'The Apple' and shouted, 'Excuse me, Madame,' just before the 'Original Sin' or first bite."

"But, Eve was so intoxicatingly engrossed, so enthused and relished in the process that she didn't notice or see him, and she almost bit Ebenezer's head off. In fact, Grampa was too slow as he lost his tail in the inevitable act. Thus, curiosity is the 'Original Sin', which led to the 'Logical Fall of Mankind' per 'Choice' or 'Free Will'."

The boys just shook their head in shock. They had heard Bible stories before, but never this one. Oouey smiled and continued with his story.

"Some say it was a miracle that he didn't lose his life in this historic event. But, perhaps God did have mercy on poor ol' Gramps, since he was on a sacred mission — actually trying to warn both Adam and Eve with a slice of advice. For he knew of God's little secret. He knew that if man indulged in the 'Apple of Good and Evil', then man must also partake of the 'Tree of Eternal Life.'"

"Unfortunately, since he didn't succeed in averting the misdeed, evil manifested and Grampa grew aghast. To make amends, he spent the rest of his life trying to get both Adam's and Eve's attention. But, they were too proud and salacious to listen, and evil persisted and escalated. Thus, on his deathbed — in front of his entire family, he made them all promise and take a solemn vow to erase evil and pass the word on to their offspring."

Both Chi and Jimmy were getting excited. They couldn't wait to tell Gram and Pa.

"Oh well," Oouey continued. "Now you know why 'HEART' is my mission, as I was deemed by fate, my Greatest Granddaddy's dream, his dying wish to avenge the 'Logical Fall of Man'. I must live up to his name —

'Divine Help' as an ambassador of God in the name of Grampa Ebenezer. I must carry the 'Torch of Truth' and deliver mankind from evil."

"I am proud to have you boys join me, as we are all part and parcel instruments or agents of God as 'Love' is the 'Way'. Man must unite his left brain — 'Intellect' — with his right brain — 'Intuition', (the 'Tree of Eternal Life'), by trusting his 'Heart'."

"Let your 'Conscience' be your 'Guide'. Your 'Heart' knows right from wrong! Humans must practice kindness, mercy and compassion instead of anger, hatred and revenge. God's secret is no mystery. Intuition is God's little secret!"

"Pa said that 'Intuition is our own Special Power! Chi exclaimed out loud.

"Magical Super Power!" Jimmy was elated.

"Right on", Oouey shouted with a big smile on his little face. "Your Pa is absolutely right. Intuition is your sixth sense! That is what my Greatest Grandpa Ebenezer was trying to advise Adam and Eve about! But they wouldn't listen and unfortunately today, most people still ignore their 'Intuition'. They don't trust it? They don't use their Right-brain? Sheer stupidity it is, so bizarre, so absurd?"

"D.T.D.", Chi exclaimed as Jimmy joined in! "D.T.D., D.T.D., D.T.D!" The boys jokingly echoed.

"Uh, Dee Tee Dee;" Oouey was puzzled as he

twisted his mustache with his thumb and index finger? Actually, he assumed that they were singing some sort of silly song? But he didn't know why.

"Da...da...dumber than dirt", Jimmy stuttered as Oouey busted out laughing.

"Pa always says that when people do stupid things; 'they must have rocks in their head!'" Chi elaborated. "They are dumber than dirt."

"Rocks for brains," Oouey laughed again as did Chi and Jimmy.

"Pa told us that we have to use our brain," Jimmy interrupted; "'Think before you do something stu...stu...stupid!'"

"Snake-eyes, craps," Chi added. "He said that life is one big gamble which is full of risks but stupidity, is a loser. He told us that we must learn to think for our selves and not to become robots, but he never told us that we have two brains?"

"That's because you only have one brain with two sides." Oouey enlightened, "Your left side or left brain and your right side or right brain. There have been a lot of scientific studies done and as a result, there are a lot of theories regarding their functions. But humans must learn to utilize or shall I clarify, unite both sides."

"Intuition, your 'Magical Super Power', is on your right side. Trust the voice in your Heart; your

'Natural Instinct', it's a 'No-Brainer'! Guilt is such an ugly feeling? Always remember that, your 'Heart', knows right from wrong! By using both sides of your brain, you activate your 'Conscience'. Let your 'Conscience' be your 'Guide'!"

Oouey paused from his sermon / lecture and asked Chi to please get him a drink of cider. Chi obliged, as Jimmy handed him the big mug from the floor. When Chi returned, Oouey took a long refreshing drink, burped, and excused himself. Then he asked the boys if they were ready, willing, and able to B4HEART.

Both Chi and Jimmy agreed wholeheartedly.

Oouey told them that B4HEART was their mission and that their motto and oath were adopted from an old friend of his. 'Peace Pilgrim' was her name, but unfortunately, she died a few years back.

"Repeat after me," Oouey continued with the oath or solemn promise. "I promise," and the boys did as he said: "I promise to overcome evil with Good, falsehood with Truth, and hatred with LOVE."

When they finished, Oouey congratulated them both and told them that he was going to get them B4HEART badges and T-shirts as they were official members of his club. They were tickled pink, but Jimmy was still a bit curious.

"Do you have any family?"

"But of course!" he replied with pride. "I have a wife, Olga, who is as beautiful as the sunset, and twenty-three wonderful children — Billy, Brandie, Jamie, ChiChi, JimJim, Nicky, Nate, and Mayan. Then there is Nelson, Chubby, Bobby, Susie, Stubby, Helen, Davey, Mikey, Viola, Charlie, Cheyenne, Tiny-Tim, Vinnie, Justin and Baby Gooey. And, Olga is pregnant with twins."

Both Chi and Jimmy were surprised that Oouey had two sons that had the same name as them? They giggled in anticipation of meeting them all. But suddenly, Oouey began to cry. The boys were startled. "What's the matter?" they echoed simultaneously.

"I had one more son, but he died," Oouey explained sadly. The boys could relate to death, sort of, since they both had lost a pet or two. They felt sorry for Oouey. They felt his grief.

"What happened?" Chi asked sympathetically.

"Ebenezer the Second, my oldest son, died of a drug overdose, as he hung out with a bad crowd," Oouey choked out with tears rolling down his small face.

"I named him after my Greatest Grandpa, whom I told you boys about." Oouey was proud as he wiped the tear drops from his eyes with both of his little hands.

Chi and Jimmy were stunned as reality set in. For Pa always warned them about drugs and bad crowds. He insisted that they both led to trouble.

"Pa told us all about peer-pressure, temptation and curiosity!" Chi thought out loud with instilled confidence.

"Drugs are evil." Jimmy was now convinced of that as a fact.

"Yepper," Oouey agreed wholeheartedly.

"Why doesn't God get rid of all the drugs?" Chi asked, as he felt so sad for poor Oouey.

"Some people believe that God is dead, others don't believe that He exists or ever existed? Ironically, most humans invoke or call upon God only when they are desperate or in trouble. But, God lets mankind deal with most of his problems. Men must decide and choose how to deal with evil." Oouey got his composure back.

"Sometimes," he continued, "People do stupid things? Sometimes, worms do stupid things? So many humans are clueless. They don't realize that they have the 'Power' by the 'Action' they 'Choose', of being little gods / angles or little devils. Little angelic gods spread 'Hope', through 'Love'; while little devils spread 'Evil', through 'Ignorance'."

"Evil ain't Cool. It hurt you, Oou…Oou…Oouey?" Jimmy shouted as sure as he could be.

"There is a lot of evil in this world," Oouey agreed.

"Drugs are just one example, but it is mankind who pushes and controls them. Unfortunately," Oouey continued, "many humans will do anything for money; especially, if and when they are desperate or lazy and want a fast buck. Especially when governments, corporations, politics and lobbyists are involved as they are blinded by greed and ignore the 'Truth'--- that everything is 'Interconnected'?"

"Is it any small wonder that we are facing climate change;" Oouey asked? "'Global Warming'; evidently, it is profit before principle? Thus, existence as we know it; is subject to change."

The boys heard all about 'Global Warming' on TV but Oouey's lecture was getting deep. But then again, Oouey also knew that they were like little sponges that absorbed without thinking.

"Pa said that money is the route to evil," Chi butted in.

"Perhaps it is," Oouey answered. "But man made it that way. 'Evil' is 'Live', spelled back-words; it is merely wrong living. Mankind worships money, supply and demand as money makes their world go round in an organized chaos."

"Cha…cha…chaaoss?" Jimmy was confused.

"Confusion," Oouey answered, "The whole world is in a state of disarray, a little hell on Earth? Mankind denies evil as if it doesn't exist? Unfortunately, when something doesn't make dollars, it doesn't make sense?

Thus people ignore evil as there is no monetary profit in taking the effort to fight it? 'Denial', is the 'Anti-Christ'. We are all 'Victims' of 'Ignorance' as evil affects everybody, everything?"

"Unfortunately, evil escalates because humans act as little devils in the name of their almighty dollar. Evil generates money. But 'devil' is merely 'Lived', spelled backwards as it is wrong living. Men create 'Evil' by acting like little 'Devils'!

Chi and Jimmy were both mad. Oouey had fired them up. They were inspired indeed! They hated evil and wanted to do something about it. But what could they do? Suddenly, Jimmy shouted, "We can be like 'Superhero's' and fight evil! We can get Harry Potter to help us! He knows magic!"

"Yeah", Chi agreed. "And after we whip evil here on Earth, we can fight it in the whole universe!"

"Bravo, bravo!" Oouey shouted. "It's our duty to get involved! Let's declare a war on drugs and evil. They are both facts of life that must be dealt with. If we don't confront them, Humanity suffers."

"Pa told us all about 'The Facts of Life'", Chi remembered.

"Yeah", Jimmy verified; "if you sna…sna…snooze, you la…la…lose!"

"The early bird catches the worm." Chi was adamant.

Oouey jumped up, rolled his eyes in silence and looked up at the rafters in the ceiling of barn; scouting for birds. Once he assured himself that he was safe, he changed the 'Bird' subject.

"If we snooze, Humanity will lose"; he answered. "Together we can wipe evil drugs, out of our schools and off our streets. Drugs ruin lives, and children are too young, oblivious and naïve to understand how dangerous they are. We must educate them, as well as parents, grandparents, and teachers!"

"Pa will help us!" Chi was positive. "He's got 'Courage' and he knows how to fight! He taught us a few secrets about fighting. Sometimes he said, 'you gotta fight dirty, sometimes you gotta kick em where it hurts; --- in the 'Family Jewels'!'"

Both Oouey and Jimmy busted out laughing as Chi joined them. "Of coarse he will," Oouey replied as Gram called, "Chi, Jimmy, supper is ready!"

Oouey thanked the boys for volunteering to help. They said their good-byes, but not before Oouey assured them that after their summer vacation, they could start on their mission of mercy as well as their war on the drug epidemic. He made it clear that he had to take care of a few things first.

They all agreed to meet in the Rose Garden, since the boys lived five miles from there anyway. Besides, they always went there to play, and they wanted to meet his family. He also told them to tell Pa about their

'Grand Plan'. They promised and he gave them one more slice of advice, before they went to eat dinner.

"You must learn to BELIEVE. Mankind must learn to BELIEVE in God, himself and each other. Everything is 'Interconnected'. Miracles; happen everyday --- 'Amazing Grace'. There are no such things as coincidences. Everything happens for a reason. Everybody serves a purpose. We are all but instruments or agents of God. Go forth now and make nice, make the world a better place to live in! Make a difference; spread some 'Goodwill of Happiness'!"

Chapter 5
Faith

At the dinner table, the boys were too excited to eat. "Calm down!" Pa shouted until they got their point across. Gram chalked it up to an imaginary friend, an overactive or vivid imagination, but Pa knew better.

Pa believes in miracles. Pa believes in Chi and Jimmy. And, he believes in Oouey Gooey. From experience, he knows that Oouey is unbiased, charismatic and fine-tuned; as he had had the pleasure of his company years ago. Furthermore, Pa knows that miracles happen every day. Blessed is he who sees them!

Intuitively, Oouey is a force to be reckoned with. When Oouey talks, people listen! Phenomenally, Oouey Gooey is a simple worm with a simple plan — 'LOVE'! Imagine that! For Oouey is but a 'Blessing' in a state of 'Grace'! He knows how to worm his way into your 'Heart'.

Pa laughed to himself; in spite of the fact that the world is in a sick situation. He thought about Oouey's dad, who was a friend of his dad's, but that is another story. Ironically, he figured that if a serpent was responsible for the 'Fall of Man'; then a worm, Oouey, could surely 'Enlighten' mankind!

He wished Oouey the best of luck and decided that he had better contact him as he wanted to be a part of his team! For Pa knows that it is going to be an uphill battle, a coordinated effort, since contemporary man believes in logic, questions his faith, and can't fathom or perceive miracles. Unfortunately, mankind believes in what they are led to believe?

After supper, Chi, Jimmy, Pa and Gram piled in the van and went to town. Pa gave ten dollars to both of the boys. They wanted to buy a toy at the drug store and get some ice-cream.

In front of the drug store, an old man was sitting on a bench. He had long straggly hair, a beard and his clothes were dirty, torn and tattered. On the other side of the bench, sitting on the top of the back rest, Jimmy spotted Oouey!

He got excited as he pointed and shouted: "Hi Oou...Oou...Oouey!" But Oouey didn't answer? He just winked at Jimmy? The old man thought that Jimmy had said hi to him.

Consequently, he smiled and replied: "Hello". He looked lonely as both of the boys as well as Pa and Gram noticed that he was missing some teeth and that the teeth that he did have were rotten and stained. Chi and Jimmy felt sorry for him. They realized that he was poor.

They entered the store together but suddenly both Chi and Jimmy felt guilty. They 'Trusted' their 'Intuition'! They knew that they didn't need a new toy. They also knew that the man was probably, hungry and needed a bite to eat. They looked at each other, nodded and grabbed Pa and Gram by the hand and took them to the side of the store where there were no customers.

They wanted to talk in private. Chi told them that they wanted to help the old man. Jimmy agreed as he elaborated that they didn't need any new toy today or any ice-cream either. Chi declared: "we can have some cookies and milk when we get home."

Both Gram and Pa were so proud of Chi and Jimmy but they didn't mention it. Pa assured them that it was a good idea but, he thought that giving him twenty dollars was too much. He suggested that the boys each give the man five dollars and combine their other five dollars together and get one toy that they could share. Gram insisted that she would pay for the ice-cream and everybody agreed. They bought a football and two packs of gum.

When they got outside, the old man was still there but, he was sleeping awkwardly; while sitting up. Oouey was in the same spot. It was a magic moment! Even Gram spotted him this time as he winked again and she became a 'Believer'.

The boys felt funny, they didn't want to wake him up but, Pa had an idea. He grabbed the football from the bag and told Chi to run for a pass. Chi ran and Pa through the ball to him. He caught it as Pa and Gram cheered real loud.

The old man heard all of the commotion and woke up startled. He started cheering even though he didn't know what he was cheering for. Jimmy had the ten dollars in his hand. He went up to the old man and asked: "Ex...ex...excuse me sir!" The old man looked at Jimmy as Jimmy continued; "Are you hungry?"

"My, my sonny, I sure am!"

"Ple...ple...please take this", Jimmy was nervous. The old man smiled as Oouey jumped for joy, clapping his tiny hands.

He took the money and said, "Thank you and God Bless, all of you. You all are oh so kind. You just reinforced my Faith in mankind. I may be poor but, I am very lucky as God always seems to provide for me; thanks to kind souls like you guys and gal. Unfortunately, there are millions of people all over this world that are far worse off than I am. I pray for them every night."

Pa told the old man that they were happy that they could help him. He also told him to: "Keep the Faith!" The old man promised as Chi asked him if he wanted to go for some ice-cream. He politely declined and they said their good-byes.

On the way to 'Dairy Queen', Gram told the boys that she was proud of them and Pa agreed with her whole heartedly. Pa thanked them for making a difference by 'Sacrificing' a toy and bringing a little 'Hope' and 'Joy' to the old man! Then Gram apologized to them for thinking that they had made up a tall tale, about Oouey, earlier at the supper table. They both accepted as Pa laughed out loud and said that maybe they should punish Gram for not 'Believing in Miracles'.

"No ice-cream!" Chi was mean.

"Yeah!" Jimmy agreed, "No ba...ba...banana-split for you Gram."

Suddenly Gram played her little game. Pa knew that she would follow his lead. So did the boys as she cried out; "Oh no, boo hoo, no ice-cream for me? Please I'm sorry! Please, please!"

Chi and Jimmy both shouted: "Poor Gram", as Pa laughed and she continued with her routine.

"Think I'll Go Eat Worms!"

"Nobody loves me, everybody hates me
Think I'll go and eat worms
Long ones, short ones, fat ones, thin ones
See how they wriggle and squirm

Nobody likes me, everybody hates me,
Think I'll go eat worms...
big fat juicy ones, little slimy skinny ones,

hope they don't have germs!"

Nobody likes me, everybody hates me
Think I'll go and eat worms
Long thin slimy ones, short fat fuzzy ones
Ooey gooey, ooey gooey worms

While Gram was singing, Pa laughed again as he knew that Oouey would be mildly offended if he was here, with them. The boys also laughed as they joined in as did Pa. It was a family affair!

"Nobody loves me, everybody hates me
Think I'll go and eat worms
Long ones, short ones, fat ones, thin ones
See how they wriggle and squirm

Nobody likes me, everybody hates me,
Think I'll go eat worms...
big fat juicy ones, little slimy skinny ones,
hope they don't have germs!"

Nobody likes me, everybody hates me
Think I'll go and eat worms
Long thin slimy ones, short fat fuzzy ones
Ooey gooey, ooey gooey worms

Meanwhile, as Oouey got home, he was greeted by his wife Olga and their offspring. Naturally, Olga gave him the 'Third-Degree' as well as the 'Evil-Eye'. Oouey confessed as he spilled the beans about his frightening ordeal.

"What am I gonna do with you?" Olga asked

with a frustrated look on her beautiful face.

"Love me and keep me!" Replied Oouey.

Their children all laughed. They were very pleased and elated with the outcome. They were grateful and proud of their Father, since Chi and Jimmy were going to help him fulfill their Greatest Grampa Ebenezer's death wish.

"It's about 'Time'!" Olga shouted. "Humans must suspend disbelief, listen, take heed and pass it on; --- 'The Art of Love'!" She was adamant as she insisted that: "Mankind must learn to focus, pay attention and; never underestimate the element of 'Surprise'!"

Oouey agreed as he kissed her on her forehead and told them that he had some work to do. He excused himself and headed for his den. As he was leaving, Olga assured him that she would send up a sandwich and some hot cider laced with cinnamon, since he did not come home for dinner. He opened the door, closed it behind him and sat at his desk. He looked at the picture of his deceased son hanging on the wall and began to cry.

He felt guilty, as if he had failed as a parent and wanted to prevent other parents, from facing the same tragic experience. He cherished his family and life itself which is so precious. After all, birth itself is the ultimate miracle, a Gift from God. Children are entrusted in their parents care and hopefully we do the best we can? Unfortunately, they do not come with instructions?

Oouey reminisced of the life he shared with his son, Ebenezer. They sure had some great times together. Where oh where did he go wrong? How did they lose contact and start taking each other for granted? Perhaps it was a lack of communication via a generation gap? He wished that he could have a second chance.

Suddenly, he realized that he does; twenty-three, plus. He bowed his head on his desk and Thanked God for his Family and asked for Guidance. He then Promised to Help Protect the World's Greatest Natural Resource --- our Children.

Oouey doesn't claim to be an expert. Any parent that claims to be an expert is full of 'Top Soil'. But it doesn't take a genius to observe that our Children as a whole are crying out for Help.

Suicides; are at an all time high? Far too many teenagers resort to taking drugs and or alcohol as a way of coping; lost astray, trying to find their way through life. Our city streets are loaded with young scared runaways, who support themselves through prostitution, stealing and or selling drugs? Others act out via violence because of moral degradation, and a disregard for law; street gangs?

God, where are they headed --- 'Death'? Death before they ever had a chance to 'Live'? God, where are we headed --- 'Society' as a whole, with our 'Greatest Natural Resource', our 'Future', being 'Wasted'?

To add insult to injury, in this world full of turmoil,

our children are being cheated as well as mentally, physically and sexually abused? Confronted with WW III, nuclear annihilation and massacres in our schools, coping is but a struggle; on a daily basis. Is it any wonder then; a state of denial?

Are our children not being desensitized by violence, numbed as a way of coping by accepting violence itself as routine? What's happening to our social and family values? What on Earth can parents, culture and society as a whole do before it's too late? Thank God that law enforcement officials have prevented dozens of 'Columbine' style planned, copycat massacres by other misguided youths whom are confused and or obsessed with violence, suicide and a lasting legacy of insane fame.

Oouey got his composure back and wiped the tears from his small face as he heard a knock at his door. It was Olga with his food and drink. He thanked her and said that he was starving. She replied that it was his own fault, kissed him and let him go about his business in private.

'Fault', he thought to himself, 'Blame'? It is easy to shift the blame when it comes to our children but, the bottom line is 'Trust and 'Respect'. Society in general and Parents in particular are Responsible, via 'Attitude' 'Attention' and 'Awareness'. Observation is a Blessing.

Our 'Attitude', Attention' and 'Awareness' as a whole, determines their 'Attitude' 'Attention' and 'Awareness'. Mutual 'Respect' and 'Trust' are crucial. Communication is vital. They will try, our 'Patience'.

'Influence', is constant as 'Neglect' and 'Deprivation' produce walking time bombs? Idle minds and boredom are suspects.

Thus, anger and confusion are breeding grounds for jealousy, regret and or hatred which lead to rebellion. To hell with authority; bad attitudes prevail because of a lack of attention, which lead to a lack of respect, lack of trust, lack of interest, lack of understanding, lack of hope and a lack of the real heroes. Pimps and gangs are not heroes or family. Pimps and gangs add up to zero.

Frankly, life is moving at such a fast pace; it is no wonder that our children want to grow up so fast. Especially since peer-pressure makes growing up so scary. Especially since society; authority, parents, teachers, etc. can be so demanding?

Babies are having babies as sex seems to make you 'Cool' and everybody wants to be 'Cool', fit in and be wanted and or accepted. After all, the un-cool are faced with or threatened with violence and ridiculer? Kids can be oh so cruel?

To top it off, far too many parents don't spend enough time with their kids. They are too busy eking out a living. Thus, children are left alone, unsupervised or juggled --- shuffled off from place to place like a bouncing ball? How many parents know where their kids are at, who they are with or what they are doing; at least most of the times. Sadly, how many truly care?

One parent families even make it harder to keep track of their kids. Grand parents try to step up to the plate but, that is a double generation gap? And then, we have divorce, which is another story not to mention the inter-net, which is a haven for sexual predators; that are just waiting to prey upon them.

To add fuel to the fire, 'Hardcore Rap Music' as well as aggressive video games and the glorification of acts of aggression portrayed via our main stream media; TV, movies, etc; have robbed us of a 'Generation of Progress'; via violence, anger and hatred.

We love our kids and we trust our kids but if we don't keep two eyes on them, they will find trouble! Are they smart enough to deal with it --- 'Trouble'? Are You? Are they 'Street-Smart'? Are You? Can we trust the baby-sitter? What about the day-care-center? How many day-care-centers are over crowed and under staffed?

Let's get back to our school system? By law, we entrust our children to the 'System'; public schools for those of us who can't afford private school. The 'System', is a shared responsibility; a safe, responsible, sustainable environment, right. Wrong! Besides the threat of massacres, our children are exposed to the threat of violence on a daily basic; harassment, bullying. It is hard to believe that some schools have resorted to medal detectors and, or security cameras? In fact, many teachers are afraid of some of their students.

Don't get me wrong, I am sure that school districts try to do the best that they can do to try and ensure safety for our children and teachers but they lack the funds for better surveillance. Ironically, fear and threats result in silence and silence is a form of denial. What goes on in the hallways and behind the teacher's back, is a whole new ballgame.

Unfortunately, our children have to fend for themselves as the reality is that 'Trouble', lurks constantly? Danger, danger, believe it or don't but, 80% of our high school students and 44% of our middle school students are exposed to drugs and alcohol on a weekly routine. Some students are even supplied with drugs by their depraved so called teachers not to mention gang members? Most students keep their mouth shut since they fear being labeled --- 'Rat', 'Narc' or 'Snitch'. They know the repercussions --- physical harm. Private schools have their share of 'Trouble' too; especially when it comes to drugs and alcohol. And let us not be unaware of the Catholic priests.

Sexual abuse happens in both private and public schools? Perhaps it was peer-pressure or abuse of authority but, how many students have to fight off advances or are actually raped by their fellow students and or teachers? Again, how many students keep their mouth shut? How many hush, hush law-suits are paid off under the table? Ironically, money can make like the problem went away, at least for the time being, until next time?

In this land of plenty, far too many school districts are so poor that that can't afford the basic source materials such as modern text books let alone computers? The teachers do the best that they can while working with what they do have. But, they don't have the funds or resources to sustain a 'Quality Education'?

Many teachers are underpaid. Many students don't have basic health care, not to mention, major medical, dental or mental coverage? How many children right here in the US go to school hungry or can actually look forward to a good supper later, after they get home? Thank God that some children are entitled to a free breakfast and lunch program! But, what about the children that don't qualify for the free meals; suffer quietly in silence because their parents make a dollar or two too much annually?

It is hard to imagine that our children have to endure such hazardous conditions on a daily basic. How are they supposed to learn with out-dated or sub-par source materials? How can they concentrate when they are scared, high on drugs or alcohol, hungry or sick with a head-ache because they can't afford eye-glasses, or if they have a constant tooth-ache? How many children have mental problems and don't know any better as they disrupt the entire class? Little things do mean a lot; simple basic human needs --- food, glasses, medication, etc; that many take for granted. A simple toothache, if untreated, can become abscessed and kill you.

Children are not Angles but, teachers have no real authority to discipline their students. Back in the day, when I went to school, the principle would paddle your behind if you got sent to his office. Believe it or don't; it actually worked. The fear of being paddled kept you in line or perhaps it was the fear of ridicule after the fact, by your fellow students. I was never paddled but if I was, I'm sure that my Father would have paddled the principle. Hence, no more paddling today; can you spell lawsuits?

Thank God that we have PTA's --- 'Parent Teachers Associations'. They are a beautiful thing as communication can address problems as they arise, before they get out of control. Unfortunately, the system needs more, more PTA's and more involvement as participation requires sacrifice --- time and, time is cash money.

Somehow, our government manages to have plenty of money for 'National Defense, 'National Security', aid for foreign countries, war, private contractors that are robbing us blind and a private army of mercenary goon-squads that have immunity form prosecution but, what about our 'National Disasters'??? It is so disheartening to see our fellow US citizens suffer in anguish and misery as money is squandered over seas not to mention our National Guard and its equipment that belongs here in America? And when it comes to our 'Greatest National Resource', our 'Children', our government doesn't seem to care too much about their health, welfare or education? Why?

Why don't we rebuild right here in America after a National Disaster or National Emergency? Why don't we spend our money on maintaining our infrastructure of highways and bridges that are badly in need of repair? And, why don't we invest in our 'Future' via our 'Children' whom are in fact our 'Future'?

Who the hell is going to inherit and run this country? Education is but a terrible thing to waste! I thought that state lotteries were supposed help finance education? I wonder???? How much money is squandered and robbed by those in control. When is enough, --- enough or not enough, --- too much of a burden to bear any longer?

Sadly, we wonder why the good old USA has such a high drop-out-rate. Talk about an irresponsible broken down system? Believe it or not, over the years, I met several people that actually got into high school and could not even read or write? My brother was one of them? Years later, he managed to get a GED. He met somebody who knew somebody who took the test for him? A little cash goes a long way. I wonder how many phony degrees are in the 'System'.

Anyway, those that are lucky enough to get through high school are often shocked to the reality that awaits them in college. Young adults exposed to the Brotherhood / Sisterhood; immature fraternity / sorority practices --- initiations, hazing, illegal rites that are wrong --- sex, drugs, alcohol ...???? Incidentally, I forgot to mention that some high schools practice hazing initiations not to mention gangs.

Apparently, safety is taken for granted since we are a trusting people but, safety risks are becoming extremely disturbing, frankly frightening. The so called 'System', has established institutions and policies to protect us, we the people. Ironically priority is subject to opinion. Unfortunately, money talks as corporate America flashes its cash. Lobbyists have corrupted the

'System' and thus, jeopardized our safety because of corporate greed.

Thus our 'Supply Chain', is horrifying, product safety; everything from tainted food recalls to tainted major brands of tooth paste laced with a form of anti-freeze, to dead pets and now millions of toys being recalled by a major toy giant for lead paint and unsafe magnets. Buyer 'Beware; who can we trust; the FDA? The 'Product Safety Commission', which is a farce since it lacks real authority and it is under staffed and under budgeted? The fines that they do issue amount to a slap on the wrist?

We must regulate and ensure product safety by testing and or examining imported toys for our children as well as other products that are out sourced to third world nations for cheap labor in the name of profit. We must enforce quality control in spite of greed. Accountability, accountability, accountability! Liability, liability, liability! Unfortunately, the lobbyists lobby for lax rules for testing, inspecting and or requirements which affect product safety, and ensure profit at the expense of quality; an inferior quality product.

When is enough ---- enough; profit? Has profit become more important than safety? How many deaths must it take, to change policy and ensure public safety? Perhaps we should put a special tax on corporate profit in a public safety fund. How many times will some poor citizen die, because of corporate greed and the family end up with nothing or a meager settlement? How many deaths go unnoticed?

The audacity of corporations is outrageous and unconscionable. I remember not to long ago when my kids were youngsters and a giant baby food company got caught selling baby juices that were just plain sugar water. Some mom tasted it and pursued the issue which led to finding other inferior baby food products. It was blatant fraud, big news for a while and then the story died. I am sure that the company paid some fine and even perhaps a law-suit but, they are still in business today and stronger than ever?

Alas, life as we know it in this modern day and age is fraught with danger; 'Man Made Dangers', thanks to the 'System'? In the name of the almighty dollar, public safety is inferior to profit? Unfortunately, the 'System', is Subject to Change Only when --- We are Willing to Stand Up for our Rights; 'Product Safety', a 'Safe and Efficient School System', 'Health Care for All Citizens', 'Etc....'?

Oouey has his work cut out for him but, thanks to his 'Faith', he is up to the 'Challenge'. He started to write down his plan on a piece of paper. His agenda would be inter-active. Over the years, he learned that there is strength in numbers. He knows what he has to do. He will campaign to promote the D.A.R.E. Program in our entire public school systems. He 'Believes' that 'Children', are our 'Future 'and that 'LOVE' is the 'Answer'!

Unfortunately, Oouey also believes that we are losing our children to doubt? He knows that it is vital that we gain their 'Trust' and 'Respect' back, via

'Hugs', 'Affection' and 'Quality Time'. Sometimes, we have to sacrifice our precious time --- priorities. What is more important, 'Family', partying or the job?

Sometime, we have to negotiate and compromise with our kids. Give and take, so to speak. Negotiation is an art. Nature is a Great 'Incentive'! Sometimes we have to knock them on their ass as discipline begins at home! They expect guidance! But most importantly, they need Love, patience and understanding.

Oouey is optimistic, he believes in mankind and he knows that 'Attitude', 'Attention' and 'Awareness', define 'Destiny' per 'Choices'! Humans are co-creators and define the quality of life as we know it. Humanity is but a 'Choice'.

Thus, he envisions an 'Army' of 'B4HEARTers'; an 'Army' of 'LOVE', 'Concern' and 'Compassion'. Their 'Mission', is to bring 'Joy' to the World', as 'Peace on Earth'! He knows that he has to get the B4HEART T-shirts and badges as well as hats made up. He also knows that a Web site is vital to their mission as he wants to spread the word, ---- worldwide. He decided to get www.b4heart.com and ooueygooey.com — for starters. But how should he promote it? He knows that he should 'KISS' it –Keep It Simple Stupid! But?

Suddenly, Oprah flashed in his mind! Oouey knew that Oprah Winfrey would surely help them spread the word! He began to laugh as he thought about how humans fight and argue over religion. He knows that the new theory of 'Intelligent Design' is causing controversy worldwide among religions and science.

He is determined once and for all to prove that all religions, as well as science, are basically the same; 'One Great Misunderstanding'. Ironically, 'Truth' is always subjected to 'Interpretation' and 'Debate'. Incidentally, men created religion and compromise their dignity in the name of religion? How many wars are fought in the name of religion?

Ultimately, Oouey knows that 'Life' is but a 'Process of Spiritual Evolution' en route to 'Enlightenment' as mankind evolves to a higher state of 'Moral Consciousness'! Intuition is but the 'Divine Nature of Being'. With a little help from his Friends and YOU, he believes that his Greatest Granddaddy, Grampa Ebenezer's Dream, his dying wish; will finally come true --- 'A Little Heaven on Earth!'

Please, do your part in the name of 'Love'.

B4HEART—
Humanity Envisioned And Realized Together.

Thank You!

Robert James Karpie

The End!

www.B4HEART.com is Up and Running Live.

Check it Out and Take the Pledge!

Oouey   **Olga**

The Rose Garden in Delaware Park; Buffalo, New York, where Oouey and Olga live with their twenty-three Children!

Printed in the United States
201115BV00001B/1-156/A